ILLUSTRATED CLASSICS

THE SWISS FAMILY ROBINSON

JOHANN DAVID WYSS

ADAPTED BY SAVIOUR PIROTTA · ILLUSTRATED BY LIZ MONAHAN

Sandy Creek
NEW YORK

Part 1: A Shipwreck

The storm had been raging for six days, driving our ship so far off course we had no idea where we were. Now, on the seventh day, the tempest seemed even fiercer. My four boys clung to their mother, all trying very hard to be brave.

Above us we heard a sailor shout, "Land, land." A moment later, the ship hit a rock so violently we were all thrown across the cabin. We heard a loud, ghostly creaking as the vessel started to fall apart. The captain shouted out over the roar of the wind.

"The ship is lost. To the lifeboats, everyone."

"We're lost," echoed my terrified children. I felt the same, but didn't say it.

"Stay here," I told them. "I'll see what is safest to do."

I opened the door to the cabin and forced myself up the stairs. Once outside, an enormous wave knocked me back. By the time I had fought my way up again, I could see that the lifeboats had been lowered and the ship's company was climbing into them.

"Wait for my family," I cried, but no one heard me. I tried to move forward but could not.

The remaining sailors climbed into the last lifeboat and then it plunged out of view. I tried not to panic. Through the driving rain, I could see land in the distance. Perhaps, if the ship survived the storm, we could make our way ashore.

I returned to the cabin. "The crew have left," I said to my children, "but we are not alone. God is with us and will not see us perish."

"We might survive?" cried Franz, the youngest.

"We have a good chance," I replied. "Our cabin is above water and the ship is wedged on the rocks so tightly that it cannot sink."

Elizabeth put together a simple meal, more to take the boys' minds off the danger we were in than out of hunger. After eating, the children fell asleep in their bunks. Toward dawn the storm began to die down, and by the time the boys had woken up, the sea was calm once more.

We all ventured out onto the deck, Fritz, the eldest, calling out to see if anyone else remained on the ship. No one answered. My wife looked out to land. In the distance we could see rocks topped with palm trees, but no sign of buildings.

"A deserted island," cried Franz.

"How are we going to get there?" asked Elizabeth. "Only Fritz can swim."

"We could use the food barrels to make boats and row across," said Jack, the third eldest.

I looked at the barrels still lashed to the masts. "An excellent idea," I said. "Spread out everyone, and see what useful things you can find."

Our search yielded some useful things. Fritz came back with five shotguns, powder, and shot. Ernest, my second son, returned with his hat full of nails and a hammer. Franz found a bag of fishing hooks. And Jack rescued the ship's dogs, Turk and Flora, from the captain's cabin.

"What are we to do with these dogs?" I asked.

"We shall train them to come hunting with us," said Jack. "If we're stuck on this island for a while, we might have to go hunting."

"These dogs are not the only animals on board," added Elizabeth, coming up from below deck. "There is a whole menagerie in the hold: a donkey, a ram, hens, roosters, geese, ducks, two goats, six sheep, and a pig about to have babies. I have left them all some feed where they can reach it."

We spent the rest of the day sawing the barrels in half to make eight tubs. These we lashed to a plank, creating one huge seagoing vessel. By the time we finished, it was too dark to set off to the island, so we spent the night on board.

At dawn the next morning, however, we loaded one tub with tools and ammunition and another with dried provisions from the galley and some of the hens. Then we each got into a tub and, followed by the geese, ducks, and dogs, paddled our way ashore.

The Island

The first thing we did on the island was kneel on the wet sand and thank God for sparing our lives. We had indeed come across a small paradise. The beach stretched on as far as the eye could see, backed by cliffs. Beyond it, we could see forest, thick with palm trees and greenery. The sun shone overhead out of a bright blue sky.

We unloaded the tubs, thankful for all the tools and food we had.

Jack presented me with a telescope he had rescued from the captain's cabin. "I thought it might be useful, father," he smiled.

"I think we need to put up a tent as soon as possible," said Elizabeth. "The sun is burning hot. We'll all get sunstroke."

We had brought a large piece of sailcloth with us. I found some large tree branches scattered about by the storm and, employing them as poles, soon built a tent. Our first home on the island! My children gathered moss and grass for bedding. I used some of it to build a fire. Elizabeth put a pot over it and, fetching water from a nearby spring, crumbled in some powdered soup mix she had found on the ship. It was soon boiling and the familiar smell of broth filled the air, reminding us all of our home and kitchen back in Switzerland.

The boys started exploring the beach, Fritz taking one of the guns with him. Before long, Jack returned with a lobster. He wanted to put it in the soup but my wife decided it would make a meal all on its own. We added some sea-salt to the pot however, which Ernest had found in a dried-up rock pool. Franz, not to be outdone, had found some large mussel shells for us to dip in the pot for spoons.

"Where is Fritz?" said Elizabeth when the soup was bubbling. I could tell she was anxious, but she need not have worried. A little later we heard a shout, and Fritz returned to camp. He'd caught an agouti, a sort of pig that is very common in the East Indies.

"I have had a good scout around," he said. "There is a river in the forest behind us, with all sorts of things washed up from the sea. Planks and a chest and broken barrels."

"Did you meet anyone from the ship?" I asked.

"No one," said Fritz. "I called out several times but there was no answer. I think everyone but us has died."

"May they rest in peace," said Elizabeth. "And we must make sure we survive. We owe it to them."

Night fell upon us quickly. The hens and geese all settled down to sleep and we soon followed them.

Tucked up in my grass-bed, my family asleep around me, I listened to the soothing sound of the waves outside the tent and thanked God once again for saving us.

A Journey of Discovery

The next morning it was decided that Fritz and I would go exploring, taking Turk to protect us. Elizabeth and the three younger boys would remain on the beach, with Flora to guard them.

"Bring me back some coconuts if you find any," called Franz as we set off. "I have always wanted to taste a coconut."

We crossed a stream, and soon a thick forest closed in around us.

Presently we came across a hairy, round object lying on the ground. "It's a bird nest," ventured Fritz.

I picked the thing up. "I think you'll find it's one of Franz's beloved coconuts," I said.

We cracked it open with a hatchet, but it was dry inside. Before long, however, we came across a second nut. This one was edible and we had it for lunch.

A little later we stumbled across a thicket of canes. I told Fritz to hack off a piece and hold the end to his lips. His eyes grew wide as the sap trickled onto his tongue. "It's sweet, Papa."

"It's sugar cane," I said smiling.

We journeyed on, slashing our way through thick bushes, and at last came out on a corner of the island where trees gave way to rock. We could see the ocean lying before us and a hill to our right.

We climbed the hill where, at the top, we could see for miles. I used Jack's telescope to look around, but there was no sign of human life.

It was now late afternoon, so we descended and started on our way back to camp.

"I wish we could take back a coconut for Franz," said Fritz, searching the ground around him.

I bade him look up. We had come to a grove of palm trees, each tree festooned with ripe coconuts.

"They're too high," groaned Fritz.

I pointed out the monkeys who were leaping from one palm to another. "They shall help us," I said.

I picked up a stone and hurled it up at the animals. The hairy, noisy creatures stared at us in disbelief. Then one of them ripped a coconut off the tree and threw it down at us. The others followed suit, and before long, we had enough coconuts for the whole family.

Turk, who was forging on ahead, barked wildly at something in the grass. We ran up to him and discovered it was a tiny baby monkey, lying on the grass. It looked at us with big, soulful eyes.

"It has been abandoned by its mother," I said to Fritz.

He picked it up gently. "We should take it with us," he said, "or some fierce creature will devour it."

And so we rejoined our family that evening, weighed down with gifts and a new pet. By that time we had given him a name—Knips!

Back to the Wreck

Next morning, over a breakfast of coconut milk sweetened with sugar cane, Elizabeth and I discussed our next move.

"We should build a safer home," said Elizabeth. "I heard jackals howling close to our tent last night."

"I agree," I answered. "But first I think Fritz and I should visit the wreck and salvage whatever we can find. One more storm and that ship will disappear entirely."

Fritz and I set out, and we found the ship much as we had left it. The animals on deck greeted us with loud moos and bleatings.

"Let's fill our tubs as soon as we can," I said to Fritz.

"I think we should make a sail first," said Fritz.

We fetched sailcloth and set about constructing the sail. By the time we'd made it and fashioned a mast from a pole, it was getting dark. I had agreed with Elizabeth that I'd show a white flag if we decided to stay the night. I used part of some spare sailcloth to do this and saw a fire lit in return. Everything was well on the island.

The next morning, Fritz and I explored the ship. The vessel had been carrying families sailing to start a new life in the South Sea Islands. It was full of things that would have been used to build farms and homesteads. We loaded our tubs with tools, more dried provisions, ammunition, and spare sailcloth. Fritz suggested we take useful items from the kitchen and hammocks. I agreed.

In the captain's cabin we found another telescope, more powerful than the one Jack had given me.

Fritz trained it on the water. "Father, there's a massive shark circling the rock."

I reached for my gun. "I was hoping to take the animals ashore," I said. "We must get rid of this beast."

But Fritz beat me to it, the sound of his shotgun echoing across the water.

With the shark gone, we collected all the life jackets we could find and put them on the goats and sheep. For the donkey, cow, ram, and sow, we improvised with water butts, tied to either side of them with rope. Then Fritz made a collar for each animal, to which we tied a length of rope. The animals were now ready.

As we pushed them off the boat, they all disappeared under the water for a few moments before resurfacing, spluttering and bleating. They were natural swimmers though, and soon got the hang of staying afloat.

"Let's go before another shark shows up," I said to Fritz as we grabbed hold of every rope. We tied the ends of these to our boat and sailed toward home, towing the animals behind us.

A few sharks followed us, their dark shapes slipping past the boat, but none dared attack our animals.

We docked ashore safely, Elizabeth and the younger boys rushing into the shallows to greet the animals.

"Hurrah," cried Franz. "We have a farm!"

Building a Bridge

"I went up to the river yesterday," said Elizabeth the next morning. "There are some giant mangroves there. We should build a tree house in one of them."

"It would be safer to live in the woods," I agreed. "But we'd have to build a bridge over the river to carry our belongings and animals across. I'll have to get more planks from the wreck. Meanwhile, you and the younger boys could weave baskets in which to carry our goods."

That very same day, we found the perfect tree to build a home in. It was enormous, with a thick trunk and branches that would support an entire house. The roots around it were so big and bent, they formed arches over our heads.

Jack found the ideal spot to build a bridge, with flat rocks on either side of the river. But how were we to lay the planks across the water?

Ernest suggested an idea. We secured ropes to both ends of a plank. Then I waded across the river holding one rope tightly. Now all we had to do was pull both ropes and lift the plank on to the rocks. We secured it down and added more till the bridge was wide enough to cross safely.

It was a happy family that ate supper that night.

"I propose a toast to our new bridge," said Franz.

We all held up our bowls. "To our bridge."

A Ladder up a Tree

I must admit that I was somewhat sad to leave our tent the next day. But Elizabeth was right. It would be safer to live in a tree, far above the ground.

We packed all the belongings we could take with us that day and left the rest in the tent, making sure it was closed properly with the sailcloth nailed to the ground.

Then we set out, Elizabeth and Fritz going first, with the cow and donkey following. Jack went next, leading the goats. Then came Ernest, driving the sheep, and Franz with Knips chattering away on his shoulder.

That night, we slept in our hammocks near the tree. Come morning, we were all eager to start work. Even the lowest branches in the tree were out of reach, so we had to make a ladder out of rope and sugar cane to reach them.

This we built in a day, everyone working so hard we barely stopped for lunch. Meanwhile, I told Elizabeth to make a bow and arrow out of cane and strings.

"What is it for?" asked the boys when the ladder was finished and we'd had something to eat.

"You'll see," I said.

I tied one end of a thin rope to the shaft of the arrow and the other to the top rung in the ladder. Then I took aim at the lowest branch in the tree. The arrow shot out of the bow and promptly sailed down again, leaving the rope draped over the branch.

The Tree House

The boys, guessing my intention, started pulling on the rope, and the ladder rose up the tree until it reached the lowest branch. "Hold onto the rope, boys," I said to Jack and Ernest. They obliged, and I let Franz, the lightest among us, climb up the ladder, his weight counterbalanced by his brothers' at the end of the rope. Once he'd reached the branch, he tied the ladder down. Fritz went next and nailed it to the branch. Jack and Ernest followed, and their whoops of joy as they explored the tree, clambering from branch to branch, echoed around the forest.

Our first job in the tree was to build a platform large and strong enough to take our weight. It was hard work. We needed beams to support our structure, and we had to pull them up into the tree one by one.

Once they were in place, we nailed them down and covered them with planks. Then we added walls on three sides, so that no one would fall out. Last of all, we slung sailcloth over the branches above us, nailing it down to make a roof.

The boys hoisted the hammocks up and we slung them across the branches. They felt soft and comfortable after the grass beds on the tent floor.

Elizabeth, her face full of pride and joy, smiled at me. "No mother could wish for a better home for her family."

Return to the Wreck

The following morning, I proposed to give our new home a name.

"Let's call it Tree Castle," cried Ernest.

"No, let's call it The Eagle's Nest," said Fritz.

"I like the idea of calling our home a nest," I said. "But let it be The Falcon's Nest. We'll call it Falconhurst."

"We should name all the places on the island," suggested Franz.

"Good idea," said Jack. "We'll call the tent Tentholm."

"The rock where our ship was destroyed should be Shark Island," added Fritz. "It's where I killed my first shark."

"I propose to call the bay where we came ashore Safety Bay," said Elizabeth. "It's where we found safety."

"Those are all great names. And I suggest we have the day off," I said. "It's Sunday. We should go for a walk on the beach." Later, while the boys were hunting for shells, I said to Elizabeth, "I think I must go back to the wreck. There are a lot of valuable things there we could use."

"Just seeing that broken ship gives me shivers," said Elizabeth. "It's a death trap! We nearly lost our lives on it. And I'm sure it's becoming increasingly unsafe."

She took my hand in hers and squeezed it. "But I understand there are things in it we need. So go with my blessing."

The next morning, Fritz and I set out again. We planned to bring home as much as possible, so we spent the day building a raft out of broken planks.

We loaded this with the gunner's and carpenter's chests, which were full of tools and ammunition. In the captain's cabin we discovered a third chest, full of valuable keepsakes the passengers had entrusted him with. We took it too, not for our personal use but for safekeeping.

Of greater value to us was yet another chest we found close to the porthole, its lid open to let in the light. Inside were young seedlings, all in small pots. Pear and plum trees, apple saplings, and baby vines, all trees that grow well in Europe but that we had not seen on the island. We found a large store of books, too, and two globes showing the map of the world.

Before long the raft was weighed down with goods, including sacks of corn and peas, farm implements, and even the mattress from the captain's cabin.

We fastened the raft to our boat, and hoisting up the sail, set off for home. We hadn't been gone long when Fritz spied a dark round object in the water ahead.

"It's a turtle," he cried. "Look at the size of it." He flung a lasso around its neck. The turtle sped off toward shore, dragging us along behind it.

And that's how we reached our island that day, pulled along by a giant turtle. Who knew such wonders existed?

The Pinnace

During our visit to the wreck, Fritz and I had seen a pinnace in the bulkhead, a small boat with a sail, a flat stern, and two small brass cannons. It had been taken apart for the journey, the sail rolled up tightly against the mast. Could we put it together and use it? I couldn't sleep because I was constantly thinking about it.

"I must return to the wreck and fetch it," I said to Elizabeth. "A boat like that would be very useful."

"Please, make it the last time," said Elizabeth.

"I promise," I said. But in the end, it took several trips to get all the parts of the pinnace together. We put it together in the bulkhead. When it was finally ready to sail, I had to blow a hole in the side of the wreck to get it out. But at last, sail unfurled, it was launched.

I blew up the rest of the wreck a few weeks later, too, with the last of the powder and mortar from the gunner's store. It was the only way I could get the timber from the hull and keel. We all felt sad to see it go. It was our last contact with the outside world, with our home. Only Elizabeth was happy. "That thing nearly cost us our lives," she shuddered. "I was worried sick every time one of you went on board."

Over time, we made the tree house grander, building a wooden roof and a balcony around the platform.

"I tell you what else Falconhurst needs," said Elizabeth one morning. "A proper staircase."

"It would be quite impossible to erect a staircase outside the tree, Mother," replied Ernest. "But I have noticed bees buzzing in and out of the trunk, which suggests it might be hollow. Perhaps it would be possible to build a spiral staircase inside the trunk."

"That's an excellent idea," I cried.

The tree did indeed turn out to be hollow. We set to work right away enticing the bees from inside with smoke, to a hive we made for them in a gourd. We then hollowed out a door and windows in the trunk. Working together, we soon had a staircase built. It rose to the main platform of our house.

Our first rainy season came, leaving us wet and shivering in our tree house. The monsoon ruined most of our stores in Tentholm, too, so I was determined to find a winter abode without delay. My best hope was to dig a cave in the cliffs close to Tentholm.

Once the weather improved, we started the hard work of trying to dig through the rock with picks and axes. It seemed impossible. Then one morning, Jack cried out excitedly. "Father, my chisel has penetrated the rock."

"Show me where," I asked.

The Secret Cave

Jack pointed to the hole he had made in the rock. But the air coming out of the hole was stale, perhaps even poisonous. I drew my boys back.

"We need to clear the air before we can go in," I said. "We'll fetch flares and rockets from the gunner's chest. They were meant to be distress signals but we've a better use for them now. Their fire will expel the bad air."

We fetched the ammunition and I piled the rockets in the mouth of the hole. Then we laid a trail of gunpowder and retreated to a safe distance. The explosion, when it came, was deafening.

Once the smoke cleared, we ventured in. Jack had discovered a vast cave, its walls glistening in the glow of our flashlight as if they were studded with diamonds.

"Oh look," said Ernest, Knip clinging wide-eyed to his neck. "Stalagmites and stalactites."

"No," I said, running my finger along a rock and licking it. "This is a salt cave. All these rocks and strange pillars are made of pure salt. It'll be easy to dig in this cave. We'll turn it into our winter home."

We spent most of the summer digging in the salt cave. We widened the entrance and put in doors and windows to let in the light. The inside we divided into rooms, even including a library for our beloved books.

"It's the perfect home," cried Elizabeth. "We shall call it Rockburg."

Part 2: A Strange Message

Ten years passed. The boys grew into young men, strong in mind and body. Fritz started spending a lot of time exploring the island in a canoe he'd made.

One afternoon he took me aside. "I discovered a bay full of oysters," he said. "Thinking they might harbor pearls, I was about to dive off the boat when seabirds attacked me. I struck out with the paddle and stunned an albatross, which fell into my boat. I noticed it had a rag wrapped around one of its legs. There was a message scrawled on it: *Save an unfortunate Englishwoman.* I found a piece of charcoal and scribbled an answer on the rag: *Do not despair. Help is at hand.*

"The albatross might have traveled hundreds of miles," I said.

"But the girl might be close by," cried Fritz.

"It would be unchristian to leave a woman to a despicable fate," I agreed. "You must look for her. But it's best if we keep this a secret for the moment."

That same night Fritz took off. Five days passed and I started to worry. He'd never been away so long. I decided we should all go looking for him.

Our pinnace was skirting a headland when we saw a canoe approaching. It was Fritz, safe and sound.

"Hello," I said, "is there a safe place to anchor?"

"Follow me," he replied. "I can lead you to an island where a surprise awaits."

We docked at a small island. As the boys disembarked, I confided in Elizabeth what the "surprise" might be.

"Oh, how thrilling," said Elizabeth.

By now we were all approaching a hut built roughly of sticks. A young naval officer in full uniform emerged.

"This is Edward Montrose," said Fritz.

I could tell right away that the officer was really the girl Fritz had rescued. For some reason she wanted to keep her true identity a secret. "Pleased to meet you," I said and shook her hand.

"This calls for a celebration," said Elizabeth.

The younger boys returned to the pinnace for supplies. Soon we were all eating and laughing merrily, including the officer, who kept on pretending to be a man all night.

It was only the next morning at breakfast that she announced, "I am a girl. Fritz and I decided to fool you."

"Ha," hooted the younger boys. "We knew you were a girl all along."

The young woman said her name was Jenny. She was the daughter of an English colonel stationed in India, a widower. When the colonel was recalled to England, he sailed on a military ship. Jenny embarked on a civilian one. Alas, her ship perished in a storm, leaving her the only survivor.

"We are survivors, too," said Franz. "Would you like to come and stay with us?"

Jenny smiled. "I'd love to."

The Mysterious Gun

The rainy season was much more interesting now that Jenny was with us. She began teaching us English, and we spent days and days reading books and playing games while the rain thundered outside.

When the monsoon stopped, we all began repairing our various homes. I dispatched Jack and Franz to Shark Island, where we'd built a small fort and placed the cannons from the wreck. These, we hoped, would protect us should we ever be attacked by pirates. After months of rain and high winds, the cannons would need cleaning.

Once the guns were restored to working order, the boys decided to try them out.

"One, two—there they go," I said to Elizabeth.

A moment later their fire was answered by the boom of heavy cannon, three shots one after another.

We all stood rooted to the spot. Had we really heard those sounds or were we just dreaming?

"Cannons," cried Fritz. "They're answering Jack's guns. There must be a ship close by."

He and Ernest looked at each other and then burst into a dance of joy. Up until that moment, I had never realized how much we all missed civilized life.

We returned to Rockburg that night, but no one slept. Who could our visitors be? Were they honest merchants or pirates?

By sunrise a storm blew up, which lasted for two whole days. Desperately we all prayed that the ship, whoever it belonged to, would not suffer the same fate as ours or Jenny's. Or that it would be scared off by the storm and leave without making further contact.

When at last the wind died down, Jack, Franz, and I rowed over to the fort. One, two, we fired the guns and waited for a response. For a few minutes there was no reply, and then we heard the cannons again. The ship had managed to stay close by.

We returned to shore, and Fritz and I set out in the canoe, looking for the ship. It had anchored in a bay just beyond the rocks where Fritz had rescued Jenny. It was a Brig of War, an English flag flying on its mast.

Fritz put the telescope to his eye and said, "All seems well on board, father. Shall we hail them?"

"No," I replied. "Let them not see us dressed like this, in homemade clothes like ruffians, rowing a dug-out canoe."

We returned home where we cleaned the pinnace from top to bottom. Elizabeth opened the clothes chest from the wreck and selected the cleanest uniforms for the boys. Fritz and Jack fetched the most impressive produce from our fields. Only then did we all embark on the pinnace, and, approaching the brig, hailed her.

Hellos and Good-byes

The astonishment on the captain's face when he saw us was plain to see. He welcomed us on board and his officers shook hands with us, one by one.

In his cabin, we told him our story and Jenny's.

"I am Captain Littlenose," he said. "Colonel Montrose is a dear friend of mine. When he heard I was sailing to the Indies, he begged me to cast about in the hope that Jenny might still be alive. That is why I wandered so far off the usual route."

"Thank God you did," I said. "You have found Jenny alive and well."

We dined with the captain that night. Afterward, we talked about Europe and our old life there. Each one of us had the same thing on our minds.

Did we really want to go back to Switzerland or did we want to stay here, in our new home?

Elizabeth wanted to stay. "We left our old country to help set up a new colony in the Indies," she said. "Well, we have set up a colony. And we have been happier than we ever thought possible. I can understand some of the boys wanting to return to Switzerland but if two of them choose to remain, I would happily stay. Would you?"

"Willingly," I said. "We could invite more people to join us here, too. With more settlers, this little island could become a country in its own right."

Fritz elected to leave with Jenny and make his home in England. Ernest and Jack elected to stay—and Franz?

"I wish to have a proper education," he said. "With Mother's permission, I would like to settle in Switzerland and be your ambassador."

We had only a little time to prepare for the parting. Captain Littlenose wanted to leave as soon as possible. We packed everything my children would need for their journey. To Fritz I entrusted a small fortune in pearls, corals, and spices so that he and Franz would lack nothing in Europe. I also gave Captain Littlenose all the private papers, money, and jewels I had found on the wreck, which he was to return to the families of the victims.

The day came when we had to part. Elizabeth and I stood on the beach where we had landed so many years before and watched the brig disappear toward the horizon. Ernest and Jack stood beside us, their eyes moist with tears.

"We shall see them again, won't we?" cried Jack.

"They will come and visit," I said.

"And they shall bring new people who yearn for a new life and a new beginning with us," said Elizabeth.

"Yes," said Ernest. "A wonderful new beginning. On a wonderful new island, our new country—a glorious New Switzerland."

About the Author

Johann David Wyss was born in 1743 in Berne, Switzerland. Johann was a chaplain in the Swiss army and a dedicated father. Inspired by the novel *Robinson Crusoe*, he decided to write his own shipwreck novel, which included a married couple and their four children—mirroring his own family. *The Swiss Family Robinson* was especially for his children. Through his stories he wanted to help guide his children and teach them important life skills. The book was first published in 1812. Johann David Wyss died in 1818.

Other titles in the *Illustrated Classics* series:
The Adventures of King Arthur and his Knights • *The Adventures of Tom Sawyer* • *Alice's Adventures in Wonderland* • *Anne of Green Gables* • *Black Beauty* • *Greek Myths* • *Gulliver's Travels* • *Heidi* • *Little Women* • *Peter Pan* • *Pinocchio* • *Robin Hood* • *Robinson Crusoe* • *The Secret Garden* • *Sherlock Holmes* • *The Three Musketeers* • *Treasure Island* • *White Fang* • *The Wizard of Oz* • *20,000 Leagues Under the Sea*

An Imprint of Sterling Publishing
387 Park Avenue South
New York, NY 10016

Text © 2014 by QEB Publishing, Inc.
Illustrations © 2014 by QEB Publishing, Inc.

This 2014 edition published by Sandy Creek.

ISBN 978-1-4351-5826-9

Editor: Tasha Percy • Editorial Director: Victoria Garrard • Art Director: Laura Roberts-Jensen
Designer: Rachel Clark

Manufactured in Guangdong, China
Lot #:
10 9 8 7 6 5 4 3 2 1
11/14